LUGARD'S BRIDGE

LUGARD'S BRIDGE

Stewart Brown

SEREN BOOKS
*1989

SEREN BOOKS is the book imprint of
Poetry Wales Press Ltd
Andmar House, Tondu Road, Bridgend
Mid Glamorgan

British Library Cataloguing in Publication Data

Brown, Stewart 1951-
    Lugard's bridge.
    I. Title
    821'.914

    ISBN 1-85411-013-6

Cover Painting: 'No Condition is Permanent' by Stewart Brown

*The publisher acknowledges the financial support of the
Welsh Arts Council*

Typeset in 11 point Palatino by Megaron, Cardiff
Printed by John Penry Press, Swansea

Contents

Domesticities

Counter Culture

Lugard's Bridge

This collection is dedicated to
Cilla, Douglas and Ceridwen

DOMESTICITIES

BALLOONS AT LLANDOVERY

for Douglas

Towy sparkling, twisting like a bow
round the bottleneck of market day,
chrome-and-paint flecked roads flashing like ribbons
on this holiday morning flushed with balloons.
Those champagne bubbles trailing their corks
fizz excitement in a boy whose eyes
are balloons as he gapes at the wonders
drunk on the nectar of new.

Fantastical creatures, conjuror's tricks:
first dull bales of canvas, strapped and stowed tight
then slumbering serpents bright on the grass
suddenly huge slugs, rainbowed and queasy
now billowing jelly-fish, silk men-o-war
pursued by dragons roaring for silence
finally, shimmering globes of shot sunlight
tossed by a juggler high in the air.

He does not know how to utter his awe,
his thoughts are soap bubbles popping on logic
his speech a gurgle of wondering froth.
He is scared by their noise and their bigness
and the lurching, lumbering, sagging cloth
and the ropes as thick as his thighs
and the flames that bellow, and the great men
running and shouting and tugging on wires

but his eyes are balloons of infatuation,
he will fly — not flapping and laboured
like the heron disturbed at its morning rituals,

not strapped in and wired like the pilots
whose jets scream through his boyhood's skies
but gracefully, gently, in a painted bubble
sailing the wind over Llandovery market

drifting through dream and fantasy
magic and fact as a child's mind must.
Strapped in his car-chair, jammed in the traffic
of caravans and cattle trucks that choke
the grey town now the spectacle's over
he is floating elsewhere, tracing the curve
of the sparkling Towy and the fizzing roads

tied like a bow round our bottleneck.

GROWING PAINS

I. Temper Temper

Words clench in his mouth.
He is three years old and knows
what he wants, and when,
Now! Now! NOW!

He knows their 'later on' and
'tomorrow' mean *never*.
Already he could cite their lies
beyond number

if only the words would come out.
So he screams and he kicks
and he throws himself about
till one of them

quiets him down with a slap.
He knows that will start them
shouting at each other, rage
blustering

into exasperation.
He sobs inconsolably . . .
and grins through his tears
like an imp.

II. Mimic Man

In language we notice it first, *bad words*
that shock the prim librarian, the visiting great aunt.
'Bloody 'ell!' 'Oh Christ!' 'Just bugger off!' squawks
darling Pretty Boy perched on my shoulder.
'Who's taught him that? Not me!' His blushing
Mum growls righteously, biting back a curse.

Then in gestures, inflections, stance,
the ink on personality's fingermarks.
Today, peeing behind bushes on our walk,
I looked down to see him, pants round his knees,
shaking his *dink* with that ancestral flourish
my father must have handed on to me . . .

observed, mimicked, zipped into identity.

III. Pope

'Mummy....
Mummy, what's the Pope?'

'Well, you know Reverend Timms in Postman Pat...'

We can see it now, the Pope-mobile in Greendale
the bodyguards flattening Ted Glen against the workshop door
Peter Fogg made honorary Nuncio.
Did Miss Hubbard see a vision of the Virgin on the hill
Or Granny Dryden find the Pencaster Shroud?

His holiness bends to kiss Thompson Ground
and waves solemnly to Jess the cat.
'What a nice old gentleman,' says Pat, 'Cheerio...'

TALENTS

1

'You put down your pencil, close your eyes, and just think of anything nice"

Robert's an ace with his numbers
Richard has just learnt to read
Jack's a real star with a football
but Douglas knows how to day-dream

Sally's a whizz at computers
Alice sings 'just like a bird'
Lisa can draw like Rolf Harris
but Douglas knows how to day-dream

Maxwell was sick in assembly
Lenny went up on the stage
Sam got a star for his homework
But Douglas knows how to day-dream

Sally is bored by the story
Sam's quite fed up with the game
Jack got in trouble for talking . . .
but Douglas knows how to day-dream

2

He finds it hard to catch or kick
or throw a ball, running reduces
him to wheezes. Some nervous link
is missing or turned round, so hand
and eye and impulse won't quite click.

But can he throw a frisbee!
Twisted, spun and flicked up high
he makes it fly, he sets it free
to swoop and glide across the park.
No falconer could ever be

more careful of his charge, prouder
of his cunning, secret art.
Its subtle thermal-surfing stirs
his heart, not just that strange sensation
of control, it's when it falters,

shudders in mid flight, he loves it most,
honouring that broken impetus.
He watches it dissolving like a ghost
in the long grass and dares a smile,
the swagger in his stride a father's boast.

USK

In summer, when it trickles
through shingle and shimmers
sunlight over trout barely covered
by its stuttering spate,

it seems a charming ornament,
a sinuous ribbon of light.

But by November, when the rains
have bloated the reservoirs

and the sky is permanently slate,
the gales funnel down the valley
racing its brown, venomous flood
convulsing like a serpent,

devouring the gardens, swallowing
sheds and shuddering bridges,
splitting its skin in torques
of white water and roaring, roaring,

ROARING.

Driving home, fast, blood pressure still rising,
depressed by the day's indignities,
by minds closed at the age of sweet thirteen

and my furious inability
to crack that sheen of ignorance and swank
reflecting back, distorting back at me

my own capacity for wonder,
like the rainbow in the rearview mirror,
receding; dissolving; then out of sight.

LIKE KISSING GRANDAD

Late season's gooseberries, the bitter-sweet
of summers spent hiding under bushes
pretending not to hear increasingly
exasperated 'Come in, *now*, dear . . .'
to bed or the bus ride home.
Whichever meant my kissing Grandad,
a tickling, stubbled, damp embrace
the bittersweet of fright and tenderness.

That garden seemed as long as life
and at its end my green deceitful
sanctuary of uncut grass and thorns.
A Sunday school of tart moralities:
that knives impress round every joy,
the ripest fruits trail out of reach,
that downy babes, green innocents,
grow grizzled grandads;

sallow, veined and bitter-sweet.

ELEGY

(for Constance May Edwards 1898-1987)

Nanny, I hope that God you sang
and prayed to for so long
has a sense of humour — he'll need it
now you've gone from *Coed-yr-Ynys*,
your spick house above the river
whose heartstones fix the yuppy sprawl
that's now Llangynidr to its past.

Your memories gave the place
some meaning; bright girls adventuring
to Brecon in a cart on market days,
your father's ride each week to Merthyr,
over the tops, collecting
births and deaths for his big book
and, further back, *The Silver Trumpet*

an uncle whose fierce, sweet words
filled the chapels of the valley
for a generation . . . your thinning
silver hair recalled him to me
Connie — though I never dared
to call you so in life — that snap
of you cradling Ceridwen

on your lap, just a few weeks back,
becomes an icon, a moment
that seemed insignificant now
fixes a whole life. Named for you

our daughter has inherited
your stubborn wickedness, even,
in 'disposables', your swaggering gait.

We swore you'd see the century out.
Your Music Hall catch phrase,
'I live to aggravate you',
and that feisty laugh, banging your stick
on the floor, seemed irrepressible.
Nanny, don't be too hard on God
if things up there aren't quite up to the mark,

you kept him waiting a long time,
now you can re-arrange his dresser,
make sure the silver really shines.

MONSTERS

Two weeks to go and they are everywhere,
skulking in the crevices of imagination,
in shops, on buses, lurching down the street,
waving with that spastic affability
from their islands of unconsciousness
adrift between our civilised recoil
and our animal detestation of the maimed.

I had not thought of myself like this —
a closet Nazi obsessed by genetic imperfections —
but, unspoken, our most secret fears
feast on the poisoned clouds from Chernobyl,
on Thalidomide images inspired by
the steroid tablets and glasses of wine
she took before we knew the child was due,

and that two-headed lamb in Llanidloes museum,
stumbled on, unexplained; a monster
of innocence I couldn't see the horror in
at first — pert among stuffed foxes
as when its mother licked away the afterbirth —
but now, invading dreams, becomes
the omen which *this* monster would deny.

SPLASHES FROM THE CAULDRON

for Ceridwen

Power

Not General Bullyboy strutting his medals
    at masses of school kinds with fear in their eyes.
Not President Prayforus grey in his bunker
    nervously tapping the button marked PEACE.
Not the Lords of the Ledgers, their passionate interest
    the debts of the starving, the bonds of the meek.
Not Pope Ayatollah, preaching fat patience
    to millions whose bread is sand mixed with grief.
But those family men, those mild eyed commuters,
    the butchers, the bakers, the frail undertakers,
the husbands, the lovers, all grunters in darkness
whose Man-making spark will illumine oblivion,
struck without knowledge, spent without thought,
that instant of Godliness; shuddering; unleashed.

Positive

The egg has swallowed the moon.

It's taken. Ripening. Coming to fruit.
She's up the spout, in the club,
baking a bun in her oven.
She's generating her own futures,
a stock exchange, originating, incubating,
letting her cells divide and rule.
She's occupied territory, promied lands

Empire of some young potentate
with expansionist plans. And sick.

First pee in this tube; shake three times
say the magic words, add a dash of science.
If two brown rings appear in the mirror
CONGRATULATIONS. If you are unhappy, ring . . .

Squatter's Rites

Urine sample, blood test
pressure checked, heartbeat scanned,
smeared, swabbed, hormone rated,
most conducive diet planned
exercises, bed rest,
sickness, heartburn, swelling hands
conception and delivery dated
smokes and drink made contraband.

The rite of Love: the right to love.
The rite of Passage: the right to dream.
The rite of Blood: the right to be.
The rite of Light: the right to scream.
The rite of Terror: the right to be free.
The rite of Love: the right *to* love.

Scan

The radiographer, a bio-archaeologist,
probes her sonic scalpel through
the pale stratigraphy of your mother's flesh
briefly uncovering you, old-new fossil child,
emerging through the silt of generations
to this tv screen. You have your grandfather's
profile; asleep in his chair at seventy five
he scans the darkness you're just coming through.
What message do you bring us, little one?
The radiographer jots details on her pad,
evidence, the dusty facts; you are all there.
But as you turn and seem to wave,
sensing a window through birth's amnesia,
I fear the most important truth eludes
her crystal calculations; your signalling
in primal semaphor seemed comic,
a puppet show, pre-natal pantomime,
but something stirring in deep memory knows
you're painting pictures in Creation's cave,
terrors from the bio-darkness,
images whose meaning's lost to words, but,
encoded in the DNA like love's ancestral promise;
                            bind.

Quickening

The old wives said, when they felt
that first faint butterfly in the womb
it was the foetus come alive, becoming *quick*
as if before that act of wilfulness,
that first turning over in the crumpled bed
of flesh, the child was *not*, was just
a superior form of grit in a superior oyster,
wombstone, too often tombstone, the Spirit
might bless pearl. We scoff at such simplicities.

Today your mother said she felt you stir.
I go to find your cot up in the attic,
begin to paint your room, she sorts out clothes
and flicks through pages in *The Book of Names*
our preparations quickening, the tests confirmed.

'Mummy's got a baby in her tummy . . .'
        'Did she eat it?'

CannibMum, stirring her cooking pot
of infant stew, bang-belly-calabash
breasts like uglifruit, grunts Afro-Celtic
curses as she stomps the firelight.
She is an awesome sight, a body quite
possessed, replete with mysteries
that creak and gurgle and burn and weep.

Her shadow is a bulbous baobab,
the witches tree: squat, hollow, the gateway
to infinity, a chapel where the spirits
pass from one world to the next. She is taboo,
holy, a sacred shrine men worship at
but may not enter. Her priestesses death's
midwives, delivering souls into new life.

35 Weeks

'by now you may be feeling a little uncomfortable and beginning to be
anxious for the waiting to be over . . .'

Your whole being is pregnant now, 'lumpish'
grumpy, unable to bend in the middle
but obsessed with things that have crept
into unreachable corners. You are easily tired,
depressed, you creak when you sit down or stand
must eat at unsociable hours. Your feet
begin to swell, you can't climb up the stairs,
when you cough you will wet yourself.
You resent everything — the weather, the street lamps,
the fact that the clocks have gone back an hour,
that the baby books are all written by men
most of all the *un*pregnant, telling you
again and again, 'not long to go now, don't fret,
once it's born you won't remember any of this'.

Heart to Heart

How should I address you, little one, on the eve of your birth?
What can I say that might ease your passage through the bloody gates
     of life?
It is such a short way to travel, the thickness of your mother's flesh
out towards the light, and yet the farthest journey you will make.
I will be waiting for you; the fat, bald, bearded one, looking afraid
and in the way. I will say something conventionally clichéd
and probably cry; do not be ashamed of your old dad so soon.

This is not what I wanted to say. I wanted to talk to you seriously,
     gravely,
in a way that will not be possible tomorrow. Tonight we can speak
of the Mysteries, of the deep truths, of the real meaning of things.
Tomorrow it will be all nappies and baby blues. So, how to begin?
I feel I know you quite well already, like prisoners in adjoining cells
tapping the pipes, we've shaken hands through the womb wall,
and that brief scan, opening the grille, gave me an image to nourish,

to flesh out with the features of your tribe. But I recognise,
of course, that I invent you; I am really talking to myself.
And that is the ultimate Mystery, the deepest truth, the real reason
     why
there is finally nothing to say, except, that I will be waiting for you,
always; at the school gates, outside the party, at the station,
in your triumphs and your griefs. And later, if there's *another place*,
I'll be the fat, bald, bearded one, looking afraid and in the way.

Coming Out

A frightened mare
galloping down cobbled
streets on a stormy night;
your heartbeat fills the room.

Through the open window of the labour ward
the incinerator's smokestack looms.
But we're beyond such omens now,

all our attention focussed
on your *coming out*
in that pale blue frock of skin
with its bloody sequins;
our reluctant debutante.

Your mother, floating on 'Inspired Therapy',
launches you into your life's long ball.
You're a sensation! WOW!

And for me, no doubts,
it's love at first sight.
Your card's marked; I'm proud
to be your escort for the early dances.

This sequence was written knowing it would be set to music by Paul
Shallcross. The cantata was first performed at the 1986 Brecon Jazz
Festival.

BABY BABBLE

Cardiotocograph	Coo coo coo coo coo
Fetal heart detector	Whose a pretty girl then
Oxygen masks	Ohhh, has she got the wind?
Sterilizers, forceps	Come to Grandma
Resuscitature	Go on, smile...yeah!!
Transmission jellies	Isn't she like her Dad
Incubator	Six pounds twelve ounces, Well!!
Intravenous accelerator	Phphphphphhhhhhhh
Endobronchial suction catheter	Boo!

WITH ALL MY GRIEFS IN MY ARMS

Above Montgomery, trudging the blade
of a gale blowing thunder from England,
our small family — a blond four-summers boy
whose whining hones my middle-aged bad temper
to a saw; a baby daughter, one today,
who won't be carried but will not walk,
and 'Mum' whose love enfolds us all,
bending, laughing, cajoling joy
where we three'd settle for our selfish miseries.

It is a 'beauty spot', a tourists' plaque
describes the view for those whose eyes need names
and stories. From here you could see twelve counties,
all of Montgomery, most of Wales,
almost, it seems, to France. And up here
someone with a poet's heart sited
the county's cenotaph; a grey, unnatural
needle of stone piercing oblivion's eye.
Guiltily we sit on it, a shelter from the wind.

My son spills lemonade like a libation
while my daughter treads its boundaries in some
primal, gurgling rite. 'What's it for, Dad?
What's it do?' We mouth the usual platitudes
about the men who died, their bravery
our gratitude, the stupidity of war.
He's quickly bored and starts to fantasise
his own war games. Ptchoww! Kblamm!
He blasts the 'evil mutants' into smithereens . . .

Watching him my wife talks of conscription,
of mothers, lovers left at home,
and how we wouldn't let *him* go, we'd emigrate
or wound him in some way, bring on his asthma . . .
how anyway it wouldn't be like that again,
the mushroom cloud, the fire-next-time engulfing
everything, we'd all go up together, a family . . .
I look away, over England, down to the ford
where, since before the Romans came, young men

have fought to save their kin from strange invaders
with rough hands and tongues. I've boasted
that there's nothing I'd fight for, not flag,
religion or some abstract cause,
that choice a luxury my generation —
the first one for a thousand years
not swaddled with a bayonet — could afford.
But cradling my kids, here, on this stone,
I know that boast just empty words. I'd go,

like all the others did; not out of duty,
fear or pride, not for the bloodlust,
the excitement or the glory, not for
that fiction the movie-makers show,
but for love, that cruellest irony
the men who made this monument understood
and which, now, keeps it holy. Above
Montgomery, the wind streaming tears
down our faces, as we race the storm clouds

booming in the east.

COUNTER CULTURE

DANCE LIKE A BUTTERFLY, STING LIKE A BEE

'Walcott is the heavyweight of the black poetry game'

for Anne Walmsley

The hall is full of lights and whites
fat in tuxedos, fanning programmes.
Aficionados, promoters, his fans,
some have paid money, travelled overnight
to see him perform. All goes quiet,
then the hall erupts as the big man enters
stares at them, hitches his pants in defiance
and goes into the old routine: they stir
up his hatred, his passion, his fire . . .
He mocks them with unflinching irony
and knocks 'em cold. *Pure Poetry*
the critics write next day, *the Empire's*
Champ. His mandatory eight-counts
punchy rhymes, those subtle feints and glides
endear him to them, they rave about
his muscled form, his stunning imagery.
He is unmoved by their applause, nurses a pride
as bruised as history by his art's indignities.

TIDY

(for Paul Tambling)

If I said our trades had much in common —
poet and builder — a watery mix
of craft and guile and vanity
stiffened with the gravel of tradition

and the embarrassment of art —
you'd flash that condescending smile
which means 'he's a prat but he's a customer'
and growl, 'heavy scene, dear boy'.

If I said a poem was a kind of shelter
a space for the imagination to reside,
a structure kept together by compression —
each word a block cemented in its line,

each verse a room with windows that let light
and doors to enter by . . . that a poem
in the making needs its own scaffolding,
a sense of architecture, a feeling for design,

that, though words can be as cussed
as your 'Animals', your Merthyr labourers,
if required, I'll float a skim of rhyme
to hide a poem's snags and flaws

or hack away the ornament of past styles
to let its stones show through,
point up its unexpected character . . .
you'd laugh straight in my face.

Poets don't lug hods of concrete
up rickety ladders, don't rake
choking mortar off crumbling walls,
don't break their backs plastering

unreachable corners or crawl
into sewers, shin chimney corbels.
But poetry has its own aggravations,
its own risks, its own kind of grime.

In the end what unites us, poet
and builder, is the ambition
to make something that will survive us;
watertight, solid, 'tidy'.

BLOCKBUSTER

Three tons of logs, a hand axe
and the evenings drawing in,

a thousand bark-bound volumes
stacked, a winter's library
of fuel for the imagination
kindling hearth-side mysteries
of firelight and dream;
man's oldest reference work.

Thaak! Each knotted history
cracked along its spine,
each gnarled old plot dissected
by this steely critic's eye,
Kraak! Unruly poems metred
by his blade's strict prosody.

Ferocious reader, honed
bookmark, paring weighty tomes
into their chapters, paragraphs,
the opened pages white as bond
each sentence green and pungent
of the Author's sappy ink.

Outside the weather rages,
thunder rattles all the doors
we toss on a few more pages:
faces, windows, cities, worlds . . .
voices hissper from the flames
as shadows dance across the walls,

in the embers, happy endings,
in the ash, fate's augury.
The formula's unchanging;
our mesmeric masterpiece.

'SEE-FEELING'

for Ronald Moody

The heart's persistence generates an optimism,
that at the heart of things the known-unknown
defies reduction to the schemes of those
whose minds demand an easy, reasoned order.

The sculptor's green, black, hands confront
anarchies of meaning: in his god eye
the see-feeling disturbs complacency
until the heartwood's genius is disclosed,

holding unknown within known, for those
who know to see and in the seeing, unknow.

COUNTER CULTURE

Gaunt aesthete, the empty easel leans
in a landscape of rank grass and shrubbery,
its atmospheric canvas sublimely drawn;
torn willows front a screen of fern
and bluebells, that brief inch of sky;
see, the pigments seem to mingle in the breeze!
A super-realist this anonymous Creator
has no time for the abstractions
of art galleries, exhibits in the open air,
his work unframed and ridiculously cheap.

BOOKMARK

I fold the pages of my books,
even borrowed ones, to show me
where I am, what I applaud.

My lady disapproves, regards me
as a vandal for such wanton
despoilation, primly resents

the imposition of my hand's trail
through the starched and rustling
skirts of her chaste volumes.

I scoff at this, myself prefer
a used and worldly whore, battered
with love, to precious spinster

forever left unopened on the shelf.

WAS-BEETLE

'In perfect working order...'
each limb and wing in place,
hairs bristled on the underparts,
this fossil mocks the quick
fantastic creature it portrays
by such stony inactivity.

But what's lost? What fuel
would turn the waiting motors,
set seized bearings on their course?
What lack could be discovered
if this rigoured shell were split?

Was-beetle watches the world emerge,
seems a sweet-meat, pared chocolate
I might devour, suck its answers out
between my teeth, essences
withering tongue like strychnine,
like brilliant scuttling poetry...

FAMOUS POET

is on record, listen to the monster's
scuffed voice grating his poems out;
the angry prayers of a desolate man.
Hunched in the corner of my room he terrifies.

As if from fright the power fails
and in sudden darkness his words trail
awfully into silence, like a dying man,
all energy spent, trying desperately to sing.

ALPHOBIABET

Anthophobia or *Nurseryman's Nadir*;
fear of rabid dogweed and the snake-head's venom.

Brontophobia or *Thursday's Weather*;
fear of clouds in boxing gloves, of Shango breaking wind.

Claustrophobia or *The Nomad's Energy*;
fear of rattling key-rings and the city's padded cell.

Dendrophobia or *Macbeth's Disease*;
fear of careless lumberjacks and falling leaves.

Equophobia or *The Centaur's Dilemma*;
fear of the senses' rash stampede, of the motorcar's undoing.

Faeceophobia or *Kilroy's Fever*;
fear of nappy liners and putting one's foot in it.

Gallophobia or *The Snail's Petition*;
fear of gossamer correspondence, of exploding camemberts.

Hydrophobia or *Fire's Heel*;
a titanic fear of icebergs, of living in Wales.

Indophobia or *Raj Rejection*;
fear of dhotis and Far Pavilions.

Jargonophobia or *Sociology's Cancer*;
fear of Art Historians and the Pentagon.

Kissophobia or *The Schoolboy's Terror*;
fear of lipstick and the Judas embrace.

Languophobia or *The Mute's Psychology*;
fear of dictionaries and talking clocks.

Mursophobia or *The Mammoth's Undoing*;
fear of skirting boards and farmers' wives.

Negrophobia or *Powell's Torment*;
fear of Jesse Jackson and the Arsenal football team.

Ophidiophobia or *Eve's Legacy*;
fear of costly handbags and the final rattle.

Paddyophobia or *Paisley's Defence*;
fear of bottled Guinness and Terry Wogan.

Queenophobia or *The Republican's Senility*;
fear of postage stamps and double-headed coins.

Rhymophobia or *Modernism's Allergy*;
fear of greetings cards and poetry circles.

Sitophobia or *Obesity's Dark Sister*;
fear of hamburgers and the carnivorous cabbage.

Thantophobia or *God's Gnawing Doubt*;
fear of angels and the worm's caress.

Europhobia or *John Bull's Last Stand*;
fear of Golden Delicious and UHT.

Virginophobia or *The Whore's Obsession*;
fear of Catholic churches and unread books.

Westernophobia or *Red Indians' Revenge*;
fear of sunsets and the baked beans' lament.

Xenophobia or *Misanthrope's Bedfellow*;
fear of mirrors and manhole covers.

Youthophobia or *The Geriatric's Grimace*;
fear of acne and lollipop men.

Zenophobia or *The Yogi's Rheumatism*;
fear of wind-change and sudden diarrhoea.

TATE, AH TATE

My friend the anarchist photographer
and I
decided to collaborate;
we'd make *daguerreograms*
his images, my words,
randomly alligned;
not illustration,
not explication,
no names, no fame,
no salon games
just intrigue,
frisson,
art.

We were quite pleased with the results,
decided to donate some
to the nation
infiltrate the card racks
of the national collection
at the Tate,
our Tate.
We stamped
THIS CARD IS FREE:
NO CHARGE
across the backs
and,
generously,
slid them in among the ranks
of reproductions,
distorted snaps
of Tateart
in the gallery bookshop.

Then we stood back to wait for the response.

Folks seemed amazed
could not believe
these curious artefacts were true.
'Free?'
they quizzed bemused assistants.
The management fumed,
denied responsibility
and set to,
picking our weeds
out of their glorious garden.

This seemed to us
like recognition
so we printed more
and, every week,
renewed our bold,
anonymous
bequest
until, one afternoon,
the strong arm of official taste —
more used to nabbing shoplifters than benefactors —
disturbed us in the act.
'No more of *that!*'

Interviewed among the tat
of DADA
and old POP
(in neat gilt frames, of course)
we were accused
by the Trustees

of 'littering',
'depositing unwanted rubbish in a public pla
and told we might be banned
or brought to court.

My friend the anarchist photographer
and I
LAUGHED:
we wondered, had they got
their rubbish
and their art
confused?
(an understandable mistake)
and offered to donate
our whole collection to the Tate,
unframed it's true,
but still, we felt,
a gesture even they would understand.

And we were right.
They kicked us out.

LUGARD'S BRIDGE

LEGISLATORS

'There is nothing evil about apartheid;
as the poet said, "Good fences make good neighbours"...'

The President is clearly a man of culture,
he knows the poets have all the real power
their words have a way of twisting truth around
that's why so many books — and poets — are banned,
in case the walls come tumbling down.

WOUNDS

Outside the supermarket's glass
the city's cripples congregate
like dogs outside an abattoir,
jostling for bones . . .
The limbless and albino,
the diseased and half-insane,
all hail us as we scuttle out,
clutching our wine and chocolate,
the fixes on a life-style
they imagine's without pain.

One evening here I catch myself
selecting among disfigurements
for which should take my token coins
my guilty alms, my change.
When charity congeals
to such discreet perversions
what are these tokens token of?
Such grim transactions
have become routine, and thus
at least, a fair exchange,

a dialogue between the faceless maimed.

DAMBATA THE EUNUCH

is a ladies' man,
in his lurex turban,
his reflecting shades:
such ostentation
is discreet, a passport
to the most exclusive
chambers. A favoured
serving man — the
ambassador of passions —
trilling his praises
where *all* flattery
deceives, he is
a voyeur of the idly
intimate, perpetually
in ecstasies of anguish.
Could tell you more
of women's wiles
than any boasting
bucking ram but gelds
his tongue; counting
his blessings,
living by his lack.

BLACK LIGHTNING

Mabrak was a slave, a cypher
on that blood-stained palimpsest
which is the diaspora's shame,
its chronicle. He bore the marks
of Oyo to his grave in Morant Bay
but, spirit-child, is re-born
once each generation into rage.
His names enact a history.
Today he's doing field-work
for his dissertation: 'Luminary
Emblems in West African Folk
Art.' He has inside information,
so he says.
            A mystic, (he
hoards the texts on pyromancy,
fulgurites, the loud secrets
of percussion) though he affects
a revolutionary style,
take care you do not cross him
his temper rides a fragile fuse,
his students named him *Shango*
that is; Dread personified.

WEST INDIES, U.S.A.

Cruising at thirty thousand feet above the endless green
the islands seem like dice tossed on a casino's baize,
some come up lucky, others not. Puerto Rico takes the pot,
the Dallas of the West Indies, silver linings on the clouds
as we descend are hall-marked, San Juan glitters
like a maverick's gold ring.

            All across the Caribbean
we'd collected terminals — airports are like calling cards,
cultural fingermarks; the hand-written signs at Port-
au-Prince, Piarco's sleazy tourist art, the lethargic
contempt of the baggage boys at 'Vere Bird' in St Johns . . .
And now for plush San Juan.

            But the pilot's bland,
you're safe in my hands drawl crackles as we land,
"US regulations demand all passengers not disembarking
at San Juan stay on the plane, I repeat, stay on the plane."
Subtle Uncle Sam, afraid too many desperate blacks
might re-enslave this Island of the free,
might jump the barbed

            electric fence around 'America's
back yard' and claim that vaunted sanctuary . . . 'give me your poor . . .'
Through toughened, tinted glass the contrasts tantalise;
US patrol cars glide across the shimmering tarmac,
containered baggage trucks unload with fierce efficiency.
So soon we're climbing,

            low above the pulsing city streets;
galvanised shanties overseen by condominiums

polished Cadillacs shimmying past Rastas with pushcarts
and as we climb, San Juan's fools-glitter calls to mind
the shattered innards of a TV set that's fallen
off the back of a lorry, all painted valves and circuits
the roads like twisted wires,

                        the bright cars, micro-chips.
It's sharp and jagged and dangerous, and belonged to someone else.

TOURIST GUIDE, WEST AFRICA

Welcome to our *African Experience*
where you will see jungle and monkeys
and native village life.
As you know we Africans are full of energy,
and you see how rhythmically our women move,
even with buckets of water on their heads,
and we are very fertile, like the soil —
feel free to photograph
inside the compounds that we pass —
look, there are green monkeys
and here is Uncle John
who will climb a palm nut tree
and let you try his *jungle juice*
and *fire water* . . . feel free,
feel free, remember, you are on holidays.
When the children shout 'Toubob' and wave
they mean 'Welcome, welcome . . .
We are very glad to see you here,'
but please don't throw them coins like that —
see how they're wrestling in the dust —
we don't want them to beg.

There are four main tribes in our country
but now we inter-breed and get mixed up.
At our next stop the village women
will perform a ritual dance of welcome,
you can take photographs
and they may ask you to join in,
at the end they will pass round a calabash,
it is part of our tradition,
already they have built a clinic

with your visitors' donations.
So you see you are very welcome.
We Gambians do not believe in colour,
black or white or brown, is all the same,
but don't trust those damn Senegalese,
and our prisons are filled
with foreigners we can't afford to feed.
On the left is our National Stadium
which was built by the Chinese.
The British give education but no money . . .
Sorry, please.
Well, you see we are back on the tarmac road
so your hotels must be near by,
I hope you have enjoyed your *African Experience*,
any tips will be gratefully received,
I say, any tips will be gratefully received.

KATCHIKALI

(for Lenrie Peters)

Despite it all this is a holy place.
Despite the slums and open drains
you must pass through to reach it,
despite the ragged boys who pounce
on you, insisting they will 'guide',
despite the wire fence and garish sign
demanding FIVE DALASIS FOR INSIDE,
despite the concrete 'viewing wall',
despite the shepherd boy's transistor's bawl,
despite the Senegambian army's
distant bugle calls, despite it all
there is no doubting this is holy ground.

A sacred grove of palm, banana,
morokino trees, like a green cathedral
full of the silence of crickets and bees
surrounds the water-hole, shrouded with weeds,
staring like a green eye at Infinity.
Here desperate women come to bathe —
among crocodiles brown and indifferent as mud —
to placate the cruel gods of fertility.
And old men, no matter what faith they parade,
still come here to pray, when the moon's new.
And even the stranger, the Toubab,
with his camera and guidebook
and sceptical ways, will be changed,
for something un-speakable remains
some shadow of Peace in its shade,
some essence that is not betrayed . . .

for despite it all, this is a holy place.

HISTORY, KENSINGTON

1

Each week-day at five thirty
a bored Jamaican in a Rasta cap,
whistling whatever is *Number One*
lowers all the flags
at the Commonwealth Institute;
an Empire's Guv'nor General,
indifferent to plumes.

I expect marshall music and fireworks,
a gunboat salute from the Thames ...
but only tame pigeons
and a few wing-clipped ducks
observe this charade,
and they've seen it before,
know that nothing changes really,

just the outfit, and the tune.

2

Inside the Institute the dignitaries gather;
Ambassadors and Ministers, publishers and Press.
All tippling in honour of ...
    a name they're not quite sure of,
    whose work they've never read ...
but it's won the prize so must be good.

So when an uninvited, slightly mad
black poetess, from Wandsworth,
clambers on a table and begins to chant
    TOGETHERSIDE NOT APARTHEID
    they're quite impressed,
till the bored Jamaican, in a different hat,

bundles her, kicking and cursing, to the lift.

LUGARD'S BRIDGE

'Africa beyond reach, imaginery continent'

for Abdulrazak Gurnah

I

'Take up the White Man's Burden —
  and reap his old reward:
The blame of those ye better,
  the hate of those ye guard.'

Austere amid the chaos
of a formal garden run to bush
(its ornate web of borders, beds
and secret ways laid out by some
despairing topee'd nurseryman,
his last barricade
against the fatal lethargy of exile)
the sturdy grey suspension bridge
commissioned for Zungeru
that dislocated elbow of the Empire
where pink, perspiring ADOs —
fit and spick but lacking means,
and not *too* bright, blues
and lower seconds were just right —
were disembarked and rested,
'to acclimatise' or so the Form Book said
but really to replace that pap
the desk boys and politicos
had stuffed them with in Blighty
by initiation
in those rugged, esoteric arts
that really kept the flag aloft
in Lugard's gritty Emirate.

And then the real set-off
with bearers, Bible and ammunition belts
across the bridge and north
towards those mud-walled towns
whose dusty trade routes stitched
the fraying hem of the Sahara —
Kano, Katsina, Sokoto.
Romantic names which veiled
a life too enervating for romance;
that savage, unforgiving sun
or bristling, fevered Harmattan —
the tropics' *cold* when painted lizards
slow to stones grey as sunlight
through the emery air, and boys
turn old, white-headed wise.
Oh how the pale 'first-timer' yearned
for green and frost and marmalade
but felt himself always on parade,
emissary of a culture
and exemplar of a creed
the natives were to judge by *him*,
for once across that bridge
he was the King and they his fickle
unenamoured folk, so many
and so far between the outposts
of gentility.

       So, as Lugard taught,
discretion proved the better part
of conquest; patronise the Emirs,
cultivate their tongues,
insinuate their ways with medicine

and education. Such coy
dissembling was a liberal art;
good men at heart
the DOs meant no harm,
were just the pages of a history
whose evil lay beyond
their honest understanding.
What could be wrong with Shakespeare
quinine and the Trinity?
Deceived by duty and a simple code
they were the heirs to a mythology
whose pantheon sustained
the grand delusions of a continent:
Livingstone, Barth, Rene Caillie,
'discoverers' of a geography
whose peoples had discovered Life
and named its fiercest mysteries,
but lacking rifles
and a sufficient greed
revealed themselves as
'helpless, childlike, inarticulate folk'
desperately in need
of decent — British — government.

So good Sir Fred
that 'mean and spiteful malcontent'
handy with mules and dervishes
was sent to bridge the great divide
between such cultured innocence
and *real* life
by demonstrations of the Maxim Gun

and smokey magic-lantern slides.
But first the fun;
to pacify those turbulent, ungrateful, few
who would not see the logic
of Colonial Rule. Emirs who swore
they'd perish with a slave
between their jaws before obey
some namby-pamby white man's law;
the Holy King of Sokoto
avowed, 'twixt Lugard and Mohammed's sons
no dealings except war!'

No fool, Lugard declared
he had no quarrel with the teeming folk,
only their *alien* Emirate.
Indeed, he came, he said,
to liberate the people from oppression
fear and slavery . . . and by such lights
proceeded to extinguish those
of any who demurred
as tyrants, rebels or fanatic fools.
All this, his modest wife could boast,
in service of 'The Great Ideal . . .
an Empire to secure the world,
ruled by its finest race.'

II

'leaning on an oilbean,
lost in your legend.'

And this less than a life ago:
the old man sprawling on his cardboard rug
outside the Post Office in Kano,
tying packages with wax and string
for, it might be, some pink, perspiring
expert from the University
as DC10s scream overhead
and the roads choke on their daily bread
of Mammy Wagons, Five-Oh-Fours,
Vespas, 'Flying Pigeons', sheep,
camel trains and wailing armoured cars,
will sing of what he saw then
as a boy behind the blood-caked walls
of a fortress any fool could see
was quite impregnable,
of how they mocked at Lugard's crew
of wilting, whitening Yorubas
until his crude machine-guns slewed
the rearing rainbow wave
of legendary horsemen
to a bloodied and despairing spume
spattering the news of Kano's shame
to every dusty town between
the A and F in AFRICA.

And as he deftly twists and knots
the loose ends of his story

the old man bides his time and spits,
knows how the heresy *impatience*
chops at every white man's soul,
knows too, by heart, their still enforced
Strict Postal Regulations
and that notwithstanding sellotape
and satellite communications
no package leaves this office
he's not honoured with his thumb.

And true to type the expert squirms,
biting on his tongue;
he means no harm, a missionary
of technology or plain merchant
of the Word, enticed by curiosity
and a salaried compassion;
'An African experience'
and 'my dues to the Third World . . .'
Another plank in Lugard's Bridge
suspended now between
the pacotile of PROGRESS
and the trade in new antiques —
'See how this juju real, Masta,
you want buy dirty bronze . . .?'
between such arts of darkness
and the video elite.

He could not hide his disillusion;
where were the painted tribes, the drums,
the witchdoctors and gods
who cursed in elemental tongues?

No cosy camp-fire soirees
where Tradition's fables hummed?
Which steaming bush of ghosts
concealed Picasso's D'Avignon? Come on,
where were the cannibals, les
sauvages, the truly Africans?

Was Africa this stinking slum
of mud and rust and excrement
congealing between worlds?
This raucous brutal Limbo
where the lepers dodge Mercedes
and *Sweet Destiny's* unfurled
round every 'ghastly accident'.
Where Mammy Wagon lions roar
'NO CONDITION IS PERMANENT'
to the meek on Ayatolah Street
while children, blind or limbless,
scuff calloused stumps and hearts
among the charitable hub-caps, pleading 'Love'.
Where soaring glass-walled Ministries
encrust with clerks and bureaucrats
all polishing their vanities;
the Mallams Next-Tomorrow
and Alhajis Not-on-Seat.
Where cockroached *People's Clinics*
clot with every 'ten percent' machine
that flashes, hums or laser beams
but the sick must bring a mattress
and at least one change of blood.
Where bloated Marxcyst Governors

perform their Highlife antics
to the heart-beat of corruption
pulsed on empty oil drums.
Where God sold out to Mammon, so
InshaAllah: His will be done.

Of course the grey old-timers at the Club
are not surprised. . . .
                'Foresaw it all
dear boy, and told the clowns in Whitehall
at the time. The natives just weren't ready —
not their fault, really; though the country
is a shambles now, as you've observed.
Damn me, I'm *not* one of your Joberg Nazis
(though they at least maintain *some* order
still — things run to time — or so I've heard . . .)
but the plain fact is these jumped-up clerks
and messengers who rule the,
                so-called, Ministries —
for all their *dash* and their chauffered Mercs —
they really couldn't organise a piss up
in a brewery, and that's the rub,
they just don't quite have what it takes, up top.'

So he'd kept clear of them at first
but as adventure shrivelled to frustration
he could feel the knowing nod, that cynic smirk
when some 'young innocent' fresh off the plane
unleashed another *Guardian*-smug outburst
against 'immoral multi-national corporations'
becoming just routine, a reflex,

like that dismissive shrug and wave aside
of beggars — cripples, sick, insane —
who festered, wailing round each parking car
alert for any token of contrition.

He was ashamed to face such shades of grey
within himself until that melancholy
Kano'd day his Alabama-black colleague —
a disenchanted Panther — leaving, swore
'Thank God for Slavery!' and he was freed,
forgiven the corruption of his own
                                   race memories,
the psycho-archaeology of *his* tribe.
He could concede the secret meaning
of his schizophrenic dream — that every
well intentioned Schweitzer nursed
his atavistic Kurtz beneath the skin.

III

'LEFT HAND, GO SLOW, OH GOD HELP US'

But old ways die hard:
'the Ibos still chop man'
our Hausa landlord warns
and so reveals the forbears
of the chef whose menu offers
'Lank Cashier Hotpot'.
'And I quote, though not quite
in the author's words . . .'

Language Rules, UK
the whispered codicil of Empire
still insinuates the deference
of tongue-tied natives
to the rhetoric of true born Englishmen.
Confirmed in *our* inheritance
we are invited, please,
to lecture *them* on 'English
as a Catalyst of National Unity'
and mock the patriotic upstart
who suggests a Federal Tongue
composed, so tactfully, of Hausa nouns
Ibo verbs and Yoruba adjectives,
'and all those little words
can come from all the other tribes . . .'
Our laughter is a creaking board
on Lugard's Bridge, that relic
of an arrogance the world thought
it outgrew, enshrined within
these formal gardens (which,
abandoned to their instincts,
have resumed that lush
impenetrable darkness
tradition has bequeathed on our
'Imaginary Continent')
by sycophantic been-tos
grateful for Colonial Scholarships:
'In tribute to the founder of Nigeria'.
A monument to WAWA's irony
it spans a backwater the sheep
who use it now — still none too bright —

could step across to reach those islands
where old Lugard's ghost —
polished whiskers, blood-stained boots —
was yomping like a born again hussar.
From the revenge of Keffi to Goose Green
his Empirical philosophy won through . . .

But so much for history, time for a coup!

FOWL SELLER CAUGHT WITH
    WELL DRESSED CROW
'Such initiative and enterprise go make this nation grow'
Mechanibals toss 'spare-part' in a *Flying Coffin* stew
while witch-doctors sell Valium, the chemist
    'Toadsfootbrew'
THERE IS NO GOD BUT ALLAH, well,
        only one or two . . .
NEPA darkens all our lightness in the hot beer queue.
In the hospital the nurses will change dressings, at a price,
while the market mammies haggle over
    sacks of Oxfam rice . . .

Whali! Dis our Nijeeria goh dead on such Avar-i-i-i-ce!!

So sorry please de Mockracy done gone finish
we get indigenised Lugocracy; that is
the strong plot revolution while the weak
scrub voting fingers and turn another cheek
for HOPE again wears epaulettes and marches
    through the streets:
see how the Bar Beach vultures start to gather for a feast —

'poetic' headline from the

the fast cross-country taxis

though the initials are said

voters are made to dip their
don't vote twice.

many public executions.

General or Statesman; murderer or thief
TODAY IS ME, TOMORROW IS YOU
Rich man, poor man, beggarman, chief
DESTINY UNCHANGEABLE, WHY WORRY?

Notes on 'Lugard's Bridge'

I hope this poem works without these notes but the experi(
inspired it will be strange to most readers and the notes are
some of the more obscure references more accessible.

p. 64 'Lugard's Bridge': Frederick Lugard was Governor of N
1919. Prior to that he had seen military service in India, Sud
and Nyasaland. Then in 1894 he took a post with the Royal N
in 1900 he was made High Commissioner for Northern Nig
the policy of 'indirect rule', an apparently benign form of
none-the-less, radically distorted the political culture of nor

Lugard's Bridge is the small suspension bridge that cross
administrative headquarters at Zungeru, across which he and
have walked when setting out for their tours of duty in the n
is also the way that all contemporary British expatriates v
'enter' the country. It has been moved to Kaduna where it is
less, as an historical relic.

p. 64 'Africa's beyond reach, . . .': Jean Paul Sartre in hisintrod
anthology of African writing, *Orphee Noir*.

p. 64 'Take up the White Man's Burden': from Rudyard Kipli
title.

p. 64 'Zungeru': Lugard's Administrative Headquarters wh
Commissioner for Northern Nigeria.

p. 64 'ADOs': Assistant District Officers.

p. 65 'Harmattan': the wind that blows dust and 'cold' south
every year.

p. 66 'Shakespeare/quinine and the Trinity': although the poli(
to allow/encourage local religions, inevitably the culture an
colonisers *infected* the indigenous cultures.

p. 68 'leaning on an oilbean': Christopher Okigbo, 'The
'Heavensgate'.

government.

p. 74 'FOWL SELLER CAUGHT . . .': a typically
Nigerian popular press.

p. 74 *'Flying Coffin'*: the gruesome nickname given
that, too often, provide a quick route to the afterl

p. 74 'NEPA': The Nigerian Electrical Power Agen
to stand for 'Never Eny Power Again'.

p. 74 'Scrub voting fingers': in Nigerian elections tl
fingers in indelible ink as a way of ensuring that

p. 74 'Bar Beach': the notorious Lagos beach, site

Acknowledgements

Acknowledgements are due to the following magazines and anthologies where many of these poems first appeared:

Anglo-Welsh Review, Bananas, Catalyst Press Poemcards, Hubbub, Kyk-Over-Al, New Voices, Oxford Poetry, Picture: Welsh Poets (Gwent College/Seren Books), *Poems from Aberystwyth* (Extra Mural Dept., U.C.W. Aberystwyth), *Poets Against Apartheid* (Wales Anti-Apartheid Movement), *Poetry Wales, Planet, Reynard, South-East Arts Review, South West Review, Specimens* (Sceptre Press), *Walter Rodney, Poetic Tributes* (Bogle l'Overture), *Wasafiri, West Africa, Workshop New Poetry.*

'Lugard's Bridge' first appeared in the pamphlet *The Perfume of Decay* published by Alan Tarling's Poet & Printer Press in 1985.